The Three Bears

Retold by Emma Bailey
Illustrated by Yuri Salzman

Published by Peter Haddock Ltd., Brid
© 1989 Joshua Morris Publishin
Printed in China

D1439582

Once upon a time there were three bears—a great big Papa Bear, a medium-sized Mama Bear, and a little Baby Bear.

One morning, Mama Bear cooked some cereal. Papa Bear took one taste and growled, "This cereal is too hot!"

"We'll wait to eat it until it cools off," said
Mama Bear.

"Let's go for a walk in the woods," said Baby
Bear. And so they did.

A little girl named Goldilocks was also out walking. She had wandered off the path and was far from home. How glad she was to find the Bears' little house! She opened the door and walked right in!

Goldilocks saw the three bowls of cereal on the table. "I'll just taste it" she thought. Goldilocks tried a spoonful of cereal out of Papa Bear's great big bowl, but she dropped it saying, "This cereal is too hot!"

Then Goldilocks dipped a spoon into Mama Bear's medium-sized bowl. "This cereal is too cold!" she said. Next Goldilocks tasted the cereal in Baby Bear's small bowl. "This tastes just right!" she said, and she ate it *all* up!

Goldilocks wanted to rest before she went back
to the woods, so she sat down in Papa Bear's great
big chair. "This chair is too hard!" she declared.
Next Goldilocks climbed onto Mama Bear's plump
medium-sized chair but she sank into the pillows.
"This chair is too soft," she said.

Then Goldilocks noticed Baby Bear's little chair. She sat down on it, smiled and said, "This chair is just right!" She rocked the chair back and forth. Suddenly, with a loud *crack,* the chair broke, spilling Goldilocks on the floor.

Goldilocks was feeling very tired. Opening one door, she saw a bedroom with three beds in it. First she tried Papa Bear's great big bed, but it was too hard and lumpy. Next she tried Mama Bear's medium-sized bed, but it was too soft and springy.

Finally Goldilocks tried Baby Bear's small bed.
It felt just right! Goldilocks crawled under the
covers and put her head down on the pillow. In no
time at all, Goldilocks fell fast asleep.

When the three bears came back from their walk, they knew that something was wrong.

"Somebody's been eating *my* cereal," growled Papa Bear.

"Somebody's been eating *my* cereal, too," cried Mama Bear.

"Somebody's been eating *my* cereal," said Baby
Bear, "and they've eaten it all up!"

Puzzled, the three bears
looked around the room.
Suddenly Papa Bear growled,
"Somebody's been sitting in
my chair."

Mama Bear cried,
"Somebody's been sitting in
my chair."

Then Baby Bear cried,
"Somebody's been sitting in
my chair, and they've broken
it!"

They went to the bedroom. "Somebody's been
sleeping in *my* bed," growled Papa Bear.
  And somebody's been sleeping in *my* bed!"
Mama Bear cried.

"Somebody's been sleeping in *my* bed!" Baby
Bear cried, "and here she is!"
Goldilocks opened her eyes and saw the bears
looking at her in surprise.

Goldilocks leapt out of bed and ran out the door.
"I'll never go back to that part of the woods," she
declared, and she never did.